Usborne Phonics Stories

Fat cat on a mat
and other tales

Contents

What are phonics?

There are just over 40 sounds which go together to make up every single spoken word in the English language. These are called phonemes. Phonics-based reading involves linking letters – or combinations of letters – to their phonemes. Some phonemes correspond to a single letter, like the c-a-t sounds in the word "cat", and others to combinations of letters, such as the sh-ar-k sounds in the word "shark".

Synthetic phonics describes the process of reading by *sounding* the individual phonemes in a word, and then synthesizing – running them together – or *blending* them to read the whole word. Children who learn to read using synthetic phonics start by learning the individual phonemes, then soon learn to sound and blend in order to read whole words. This gives them the confidence to read unfamiliar words and tackle new texts, an important step towards independent reading.

Words can be divided into two basic groups: regular phonic words, such as "cat", which can be read by sounding and blending, and words which are wholly or partly irregular. Most words in English are regular, but some very common words, such as "the" and "was", are irregular and have to be learned. When your child meets an unfamiliar word, encourage him or her to read it regularly; children may recognize the irregularity and correct themselves, or you can guide them if necessary.

Read this story with your child, encouraging him or her to sound out the words as you go. Soon, most children will start to sound out the words for themselves. This is an excellent way of helping to develop a fundamental reading skill.

Dr. Marlynne Grant

For details of the phonic breakdown for the words in each story go to
www.usborne-quicklinks.com and enter the keywords **phonics readers**

Fat cat on a mat

There is a little yellow duck
to spot in every big picture.

Fat Cat sees a bee.

BUZZ

Fat Cat flees up a tree.
"I don't like bees!" yelps Fat Cat.

"I don't like bees and I don't like trees."

"I don't like bees *or* trees."

"Are you stuck?"
shouts Big Pig.

"Bad luck!" shouts Big Pig.

Fat Cat
groans.

"I am stuck.
It *is* bad luck,"
she moans.

The tree bends...

The nest drops,
with a plop, on
top of Big Pig.

"Like my new hat, Fat Cat?"

"Good catch!"
yelps Fat Cat.

Fat Cat lands in a sandy patch.
"I must help the eggs to hatch."

Next day,

Fat Cat will
not play.

"Play with me!" says Big Pig.

"Not today," says Fat Cat on her mat.

"Bake a cake with me," says Jake Snake.

"Not today," says Fat Cat on her mat.

"Let's run in the sun for fun," says Ted.

"Not today," says Fat Cat on her mat.

"You are lazy," says Big Pig.
"You are crazy," says Jake Snake.

"You are no fun," says Ted.

"Shh!" says
Fat Cat.

"Stay away,"
says Fat Cat.

Clever Fat Cat!

Ted in a red bed

There is a little yellow duck
to spot in every big picture.

Ted likes to shop.

Ted stops. Ted hops.
Ted smiles a big smile.

21

"I like this bed," thinks Ted.

"I like red wood. Red wood is good."

"I want to see more."

"Try the red bed," says Fred.

"Oh, yes," says Ted.

Ted slips
his feet
under
the sheet.

He flops on the pillow.

The pillow is yellow.

"I need this bed, Fred!" grins Ted.

"It is a nice price," smiles Fred.

Now it's Ted's bed, not Fred's bed.

Ted feels sleepy.
Ted falls asleep.

Ted has a dream.

He bobs down a stream.

Fred's Beds

Ted has a dream.

He bobs on a wave into a cave.

Ted has a dream.

He can
fly in the sky!

Ted has a dream.
He is back by the stream.

Ted wakes up with a snore.

He's not in the store any more.

Ted is home. His red bed is home too.

"This red bed must be a magic red bed!"

Big pig on a dig

There is a little yellow duck
to spot in every big picture.

Big Pig gets a letter.

Big Pig

Look for this hat.

Big Pig sees the hat.

There is a map in the hat.

Big Pig runs
to Fat Cat.

38

"Fat Cat! Look at the map in this hat."

"It shows where to dig, Fat Cat."

"Where to dig?
Dig for what,
Big Pig?"

"Gold!" grunts Big Pig.
"Old gold."

"But I am a cat.
Cats need to nap.
I am a napping cat."

"You dig, Big Pig.
Be a pig on a dig."

41

"Let me nap

and dream of cream."

Big Pig sees three green trees.

Big Pig sees three green trees on the map.

Big Pig is happy.

He pops on a wig.

Big Pig is happy.

He hops on a twig. He can go on a dig!

"I am a happy big pig on a dig."

"I dig down

and down

and...

What has Big Pig found...

...down in the ground?

It's Funny Bunny.

"There's no
old gold here."

Big Pig grins. "Digging is fun too!"

Hen's pens

There is a little yellow duck
to spot in every big picture.

Hen has new pens.

She has ten
new pens.

53

"When will you use your new pens, Hen?"

"Now, Brown Cow!"

"What will you draw?"

"Straw...

55

... and the big blue sky,
and a yellow bird flying by."

Hen hops
off her
nest.

"Drawing patterns is
what I like best."

She zigs and zags from left to right.

She zigs and zags all day
and night...

"What can I draw on now?" she shouts.

"Draw on your eggs!" says Brown Cow.

60

"Draw big dots on your eggs."
"Or more zigzags?" Hen begs.

Hen's zigzags are very bright indeed.

"Zigzags are just what ALL eggs need!"

...if I zigzag
all the eggs
I find."

Sorting them out
is hard to fix.

Hen has made a bad mistake.
That's not her chick.

It's a baby snake!

Fox on a box

PRIZE

There is a little yellow duck
to spot in every big picture.

Hungry Fox spots
a box.

Hungry Fox
hops onto
the box.

He tries to reach...

69

Hungry Fox pushes the box.

"Now I'm as tall as the wall!" calls Fox.

SPLAT!

72

Hungry Fox pushes the box.

73

Hungry Fox sits on the box.

But a tug from Duck
means he's out
of luck.

SPLAT!

Hungry Fox
is on the box.

"I can reach the cooling pies!" cries Fox.

But Pup and
Fat Cat ...

PRIZE

...put a stop to that.

Hungry Fox falls
into the box.

He heaves
himself out…

"I'm back in the box!"

shouts Happy Fox.

Frog on a log

There is a little yellow duck
to spot in every big picture.

Frog sits on his log
by the bog.

With one big hop,
he jumps over
the bog.

Off he goes! Frog likes to jog.

"I'm a jogging frog
from the log
by the bog."

Frog's jogging has ended.
It is foggy.

Out of the fog
runs Pup the dog.

Pup can't see.

He bumps into Frog's log.

Frog is back up on his log. Along trots Big Pig in the fog.

Pig is looking for
Pup the dog.

Now he bumps into Frog's log...

Next day, it is sunny.

"Bump into my log!" says Frog.

Is Frog trying to be funny?

"Bump your log!"
barks Pup the dog.

"You will not call us silly dog and hog?"

"No, bump away!" croaks grinning Frog.
"I cannot fall off. I'm strapped to my log."

So Big Pig and Pup the dog
bump into the log...

...which tips back into the bog...

...taking with it foolish Frog.

Frog is agog.

"Now it is me who is silly. A silly frog!"

Ted's shed

There is a little yellow duck
to spot in every big picture.

Meet Ted. Ted likes red.

Even Ted's shed is a red shed.

Today, Ted's bed goes into the shed.

"What are you doing, Ted?" asks Fred.

"Wait and see," says Ted.

Up on his stool, Ted gets down his tools.

He puts in a paw,
and pulls out
a saw.

Ted looks at
his drawing.

Ted saws into a big, round log.

"What are you up to?"
asks Pup the dog.

"Wait and see," says Ted.

He saws off a big, round slice.
"This wood is good. This slice is nice."

Now Ted saws off slice after slice.

Look who's watching – a pair of mice!

Next, Ted hunts for his jar of nails.

The jar
is empty...

NAILS

...apart from
a snail.

111

Ted and his team work on in the sun.

They huff...

...and they puff...

...but it's lots of fun!

Fred and Pup ask, "What's this all about?"

"Just wait and see!" the others shout.

Did you spot Ted's clever plan?

His red shed is now a caravan!

Sam sheep can't sleep

There is a little yellow duck
to spot in every big picture.

Sam Sheep can't sleep.

Sam Sheep gets up.

He wakes up Pup.

Pup barks. "It's late. It's dark."

"Go to sleep, Sam Sheep!"

"I can't sleep," says Sam Sheep.
"I need to see Fat Cat."

"Fat Cat can sleep for weeks and weeks!"

119

Fat Cat's on her sleeping mat in the park.
Pup barks.

"It's late. It's dark. Go to sleep!"
"Sorry," barks Pup. "Sam Sheep can't sleep."

"You need to see Ted in his red bed."

Ted is asleep in his red bed.

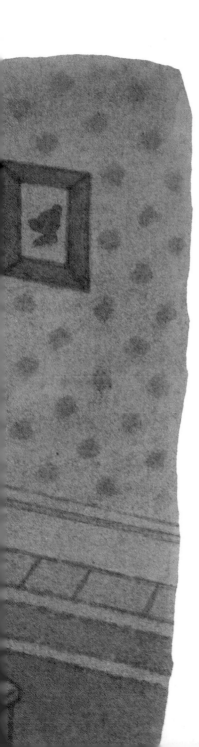

Pup barks in the
dark night ...

"You gave me a fright!"

"Sorry," barks Pup. "Sam Sheep can't sleep."

"Then let's see Big Pig, down the street."

Big Pig grunts "You woke me up!"
Fat Cat yawns. "Don't blame us."

"Sorry," barks Pup. "Sam Sheep can't sleep."

"Can't sleep?" says Big Pig. "Then do a jig."

"That will make you sleep, Sam Sheep."

So Pup starts to jiggle.

Fat Cat starts to wiggle.

Ted does a wriggle.

But what about Sam Sheep?

Sam Sheep is asleep!

Shark in the park

There is a little yellow duck
to spot in every big picture.

Pup is in the park.

"There's a shark in the park!" Pup barks.

Pup
wakes
Fat Cat.

She meows,
"Why did
you bark?"

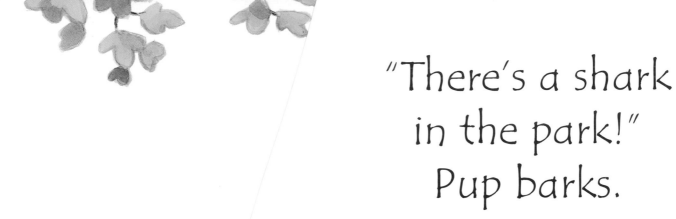

"There's a shark
in the park!"
Pup barks.

Big Pig is lighting a fire.
What a bright spark!

"There's a shark
in the park!"
Pup barks.

Hen is with her pad and pens.
She makes bright squiggles
and marks.

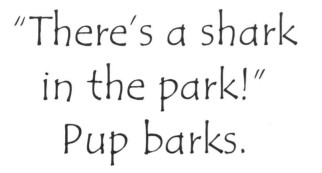

"There's a shark
in the park!"
Pup barks.

"It has sharp,
pointy...

Sam Sheep is asleep,
where it's dark.

140

"There's a shark in the park!" Pup barks.

"A shark?" meows Fat Cat.

"A shark?" grunts Big Pig.

142

"A shark?" clucks Hen.

"ZZZZZZ," snores Sam Sheep (still fast asleep).

"Yes, a shark. There's a SHARK in the PARK!" Pup barks.

"Make your way to the lake!"

Up pops Jake Snake.

There's no shark in the park!

It's Jake Snake and his rubber ring!

Toad makes a road

There is a little yellow duck
to spot in every big picture.

Toad hops happily.
She has a new house on the hill.

"My new house is best," she boasts.

Toad waits and waits for the truck to bring her things.

Time ticks on ...

Is the truck stuck?

Toad hops down
the hill.

She's in luck.
There's the truck.

"I can't get up the hill. The load will spill."

There's no track for the truck.

So, Toad brings her things up the hill.

Toad is tired.
With one last hop
she flops into bed...

Next day, Toad eats toast.
"Today is my party!"

But only Billy the goat gets up the hill.

"It's far too steep,
except for me
or a sheep."

"What you need
is a road, Toad."

"If I need a road, then I'll make a road!"
says Toad.

"But toads can't make roads," says Billy. "That's silly."

"Wait and see!" says Toad.

Toad clears a track.

She lays black,
sticky tar.

Then she rolls it flat.

Toad's road is ready.

Now Toad's in luck.
Here comes the truck!

Goose on the loose

There is a little yellow duck
to spot in every big picture.

Goose is on a scooter.
She can't stay and play.

She's a goose on the loose.
"Get out of my way!"

HONK!

She almost runs down Rooster Ron.

"Get out of my way!"
Goose goes scooting on.

167

Goose is scooting to Ted's shed...

"Look out, behind you.
Watch out, Ted!"

Goose goes scooting down the road.

She almost scoots
right into Toad.

The cows all moo.

The doves all coo.

173

Look out! Goose is on the loose.

She upsets a bunch of kangaroos...

...and shocks a flock of cockatoos.

There are shouts of "hiss!"
and shouts of "boo!"

Then snarls and howls
and a hullabaloo.

"Goose must be stopped! What shall we do?"

But Goose has stopped, and feels a fool.

She's landed in the penguin pool!

Mouse moves house

There is a little yellow duck
to spot in every big picture.

Mack the mouse is
moving house.

Mack packs his backpack.

Now Mack packs his plates.

182

Here is Mack's friend Jack.

183

Together, Mack and
Jack pack and pack.

Jack packs Mack's nick-nacks in a black sack.

It's time to pack
the pictures.

and they stack...

Mack and
Jack pack...

Now Mack is all packed.

"That's that!" says Jack.

Jack helps Mack
put his backpack
on his back.

Mack opens his
door and walks
out onto
the floor.

But Mack stays out.

He chats with the cat.

"Come here, Jack. Meet my friend Fat Cat."

Mack the mouse
is moving house
on Fat Cat's back!